To the Kollai's
From Safia Rabbani
2007

This Sunbear 🐻 Book belongs to:

_____

ISBN 981-05-2343-2

Published by:
SUNBEAR PUBLISHING PTE. LTD.

© SUNBEAR PUBLISHING PTE. LTD.

First published 2004
Reprint 2006

Printed in Singapore

SASHA
visits
SENTOSA ISLAND

Illustrated by Alpana
Written by Shamini

Book Four: Sasha in Singapore

Sasha is on her way to Sentosa.

She is going there by cable car!

Sasha has a magnificent view of the city of Singapore and its busy port.

Ships from all over the world load and unload their cargo at the port.

Can you see the cranes used to lift the heavy cargo?

It is a warm, sunny day.

Mamma takes Sasha to the beach.

Sasha builds a sandcastle with the help of two friends!

Can you see the ships on the horizon?

They are on their way to the port!

Sasha has a bag of fish food.

She is going to feed the multi-coloured koi!

The fish are crowding around her excitedly.

They must be hungry!

Mamma hires a bicycle and takes Sasha for a ride!

It is such fun whizzing along the bicycle path with Mamma!

Sasha is wearing a safety helmet.

Children should always wear helmets when riding bicycles!

Mamma takes Sasha to the dolphin lagoon.

Sasha looks into the water.

A dolphin stops to say "hello".

Sasha bravely tries to pat him!

Another dolphin leaps out of the water
and high into the air.

That looks like fun!

Sasha goes for a nature walk.

There is a sign that says "peacocks crossing".

But all Sasha can see is a monitor lizard waiting to cross the path!

There is a monkey sitting on a tree.

Can you see him?

Sasha rides on the walkway through Underwater World.

It is like being under the sea with water all around!

A giant stingray glides through the water.

A shark flicks its tail from side to side as it swims past.

A gentle dugong looks at Sasha curiously.

Can you see them?

The aquarium is full of bright tropical fish!

They dart in and out of the coral.

Sasha is fascinated by the colours.

She spots two orange and white striped clown fish!

Can you see them?

Sasha and Mamma make a last stop at the butterfly park.

There are hundreds of exotic butterflies!

Sasha spots a bright blue butterfly and a black and green butterfly.

There is a caterpillar hiding on a leaf.

Can you see it?

The caterpillar will transform into a beautiful butterfly one day!

Sasha and Mamma are on the monorail train.

Sasha looks out of the window at the lush green forest.

She sees a huge statue!

"What is that, Mamma?"

"It is the Merlion, Sasha!"

Sasha waves goodbye to the Merlion.

It is time to go home now.

Sasha can't wait to visit Sentosa again!

Other Sunbear Books
available in this series:

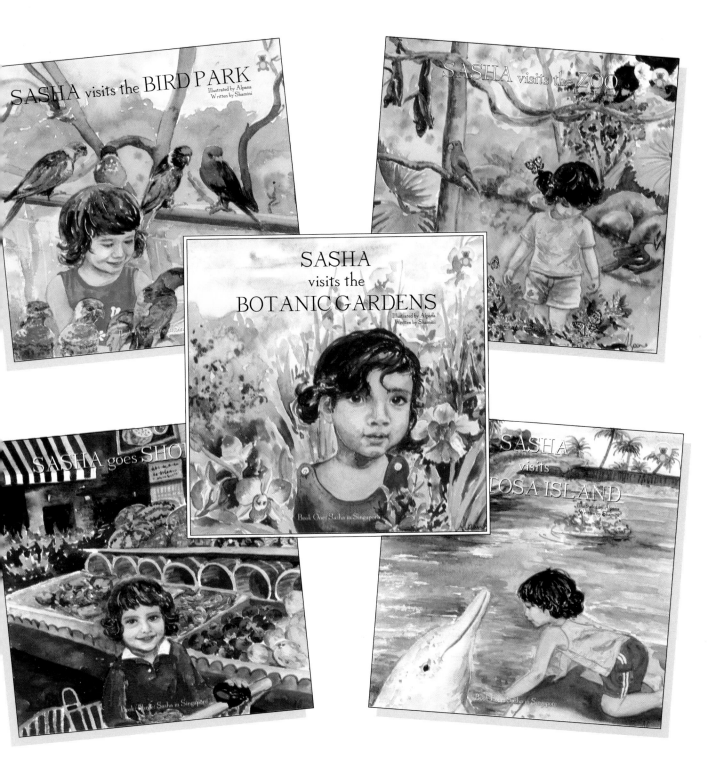